SHORT STORIES FROM EVERYDAY LIFE

ANJALI TAMHANE

The images in the book are designed by 'Freepik'

Contents

Synopsis

In 'Short Stories from Everyday Life,' readers are taken on a delightful journey through the ordinary yet extraordinary moments that make up our daily existence. Through her engaging storytelling, Tamhane captures the beauty and complexity found in the seemingly mundane aspects of life. Each tale is a window into the human experience, offering insight and poignant reflections that resonate with readers of all backgrounds. With a keen eye for detail and a deep appreciation for the small joys that often go unnoticed, Tamhane's collection of short stories is a celebration of the richness and depth of everyday life. Join her as she explores the subtle nuances of human relationships, the quirks of human nature, and the magic hidden within the seemingly ordinary moments that shape our lives. 'Short Stories from Everyday Life' is a heartfelt reminder that there is beauty to be found in every corner of our world, if only we take the time to look.

ONE

The Toolbox

Mayur had spotted the toolbox that he wanted to gift his father, at K-mart. It was just the thing his father would appreciate. It had a hammer, a plier, an electric drill and saw, and even spanners, screws, and nails of different sizes. His father loved pottering around the house doing things made of wood. He had made a very functional wooden stand for his mom, from the teak wood planks that came out of their old bed when they replaced it. All her electronic kitchen gadgets, the mixer, toaster, microwave oven, grinder fitted perfectly on that stand. The best part was that he made a wooden grill behind, so that all the wires passed through it to connect to the electric source, without being seen. But he had to put in too much effort, with his basic carpentry tools like the blunt saw and hand drill.

Mayur had first noticed the toolbox in a 'Consumer Distributing Catalogue.' But it was just too expensive. As a student, who had just graduated and looking for a job, he could not afford it. But the pleasure of going home as a graduate, with a special gift for his father was irresistible.

One Saturday evening, he emptied the contents of his mailbox, and found a lot of discount pamphlets. K-Mart was having a red balloon sale that week-end. They had put up pictures of items which had a discount of up to fifty percent. The coveted tool box was on sale too. Mayur was eager. He decided that he would go the next day, being a Sunday and buy it. Unfortunately, there was a heavy snowfall the next morning. The TVs and radio warned people not to stir out of the house, if not urgent. Mayur would have still gone, but he did not have a car, and the buses got cancelled due to bad weather. He kept looking out of the window miserably.

By the time he reached K-mart on Monday, it was 3 'O clock in the afternoon. There were very few items left with red balloons. He rushed to the hardware section. All the red balloons were removed and the prices had been restored to the original highs.

He looked for the salesman, and asked, "Could you give the tool box at the 50% discounted rate today? After all the red balloon was up on it till yesterday." The salesman said he will have to ask the manager.

He came back with a stern looking, smart, well-dressed, middle-aged lady who spoke in a crisp, no-nonsense tone. She looked down at Mayur, sized him up, a ragged, coloured boy. "Can't you see that the sale is off? There is no discount now" and she walked off. Mayur was very disappointed. He looked around a bit, considered other cheaper alternatives, calculated the amount he could spare, and after a lot of diligence, decided that the Consumer distributing centre also had the same tool box, at a slightly lesser rate, so he decided to check it out.

It was still very cold. The Consumer Distributing Centre was in another mall close by, across the huge parking lot, and two blocks away. After walking a little distance, Mayur realised, he will have to run all the way, to keep himself warm. Besides, the shop closed at 6 O'clock. He had less than an hour. He rushed with the cold winds blowing across his face. He reached the Consumer Centre with very little time to spare. He headed straight for the hardware section, and desperately started looking for the tool box.

By this time, he was determined to buy it, even if it meant skipping a few meals a week. After rummaging through a lot of cheaper items and smaller boxes, he spotted the coveted toolbox lying at the back of the shelf. He quickly held it and went to the sales counter. The printed price was seventy five percent of the original price at K-Mart. When he paid, the cashier informed him, that they were charging 25% less on old items. So ultimately, he paid for the treasured toolbox, just a few dollars more than the red balloon sale price. Mayur was happy with his purchase. He was eager to gift it to his father when he went home.

The box was heavy. The weather was harsh with the cold breeze cutting across his face. He had to walk back to K-mart to catch the bus. This time he walked with the heavy box in tow. The bus stand was just outside K-Mart. By the time he reached there, he was tired and freezing and breathless. The next bus would arrive in 20 minutes. Mayur decided to wait inside K-Mart to get some warmth. He stepped through the glass door and waited in the foyer. It was crowded. There were long queues at the cash counters, and people, after making payments were dispersing off.

Mayur was standing with the box in hand, looking out of the entrance door. A minute had also not gone by, when suddenly, the lady manager pounced on him. "I did not see you pay for that box. Come to my office." She said in a harsh tone, looking formidable. She almost dragged him to her glass cabin, which overlooked the queues at the cash counter. She called two security guards inside her office. "I did not see you paying for this box." She repeated. Her admonishing demeanour shook poor Mayur to the core. "Ma'am, I bought this at the Consumer Distributing Centre, Ma'am, it is not from here." "Is it? We'll see." Her stern face was distrusting. Mayur shook like a leaf. He'd had it. This lady will not spare him.

There was no way he could prove that the box was not bought here. She was not going to come to the Consumer Distributing Centre to confirm. Oh my, will they put me in jail? What about my reputation? What will his parents think? That he stole? Fear gripped Mayur. All his father's life's savings had been put into sending Mayur to college, for a better life. Will he spend his life in jail? Even if it was for a day! How could he prove his innocence? These horrible whites!

They are biased towards coloured people. Oh! The bill, did he collect any bill/receipt from the Consumer Distributing store? Did he? Where could he have put it? Will this manager believe him? He thought not. The two security guards were looking at him with wide-eyed expressionless faces. A thousand thoughts of shame, fear, helplessness crossed his mind.

Meanwhile the manager was turning the heavy box around. She slowly turned it on all sides. It was exactly as the one K-Mart had. She turned the box a few times, then flipped the downside up, and suddenly let go of the box. "Oh, they have the Consumer Distributing store's sticker on. Take it. You may go now".

Mayur just did not understand what happened. One moment it looked as if she would never let him off, another, she was letting him go, although she had the same stern expression on her face. Mayur hurried out of the office with the box. He was too shaken up to even think any further. He walked out of K-Mart and waited outside in the cold, for the bus to arrive.

Only after he was safely in the bus, and his body had warmed up a bit, his thoughts returned. How did she release him? He turned the box around just as she had done, then flipped it. At first, he did not see anything, except the barcode, He kept turning it around in desperation, afraid that his innocence was still at stake. Suddenly, on one of the rounds, he spotted a tiny round sticker, the size of a finger point, with 'Consumer Distributing' written in the smallest font. This tiny sticker had proved his innocence, saved his reputation, and restored his self-respect. He was thankful that the country's systems were in place. He also thanked his own upbringing. That too was in place.

He was taught to value honesty and integrity, and to never give in to wrong temptations. He did not want to imagine what tensions he would have gone through in life, if the lady manager's suspicions had been true. He felt that his father deserved the toolbox even more, for the morals he had instilled in Mayur, who was equipped with the right tools to face life.

TWO

The Brown Envelope

Saran was a young and sincere IAS officer. After working in a small town for some years he was transferred to a prestigious post to Delhi. On joining he was taken aback by the lavish lifestyle led by all the staff in the Delhi office. Ajay Singh, a smooth -talking, smart, middle-aged man, who was already a part of the Delhi office, was assigned as Saran's assistant.

Saran did not have an impressive personality, but his assistant, Ajay Singh portrayed Saran as a respectable and honest officer, and this reputation preceded him wherever he went. Saran gradually realized that he held a powerful and influential position.

All the factory owners and senior executives from large corporations vied to please Saran. They would call him to inspect their stocks just before lunch, and would offer a sumptuous lunch either on their premises, or in the best of Delhi's restaurants. During these visits, there was a lot of joking, storytelling, name-dropping, and sharing interesting facts. Saran's clients would burst into laughter at even the simplest jokes he cracked.

Ajay Singh always accompanied him at the inspection rounds. After they were both well taken care of, a new product, which needed Saran's permission to start marketing, or a stuck stock which was originally rejected, was casually shown, and just before leaving, Ajay Singh would present the papers for Saran to sign, granting permission for the stock to be marketed, having met government standards. Saran grew to trust Ajay Singh and depended on him to judge what stock to pass, and licenses to issue.

One day, they visited Agarwala Industries to inspect the new cloth that was manufactured. A 100% polyester cloth was not allowed by the government to be manufactured for the normal use of the public. Any material sold for everyday use clothes had to have some amount of cotton, so that the skin could breathe. A lot of people had suffered unease and suffocation due to the combination of polyester, sweat, and heat. A blend of 80-20 percent polyester-cotton mixture was a must. As the quality improved, the percentage of the cloth was marked 70-30, 60-40, 50-50 and so on. Most manufacturers found it expensive to incorporate larger amounts of cotton as polyester was very cheap.

At the Agarwala industries, Saran noticed that the percentage of cotton was lesser than claimed. He objected. It was awkward. The owners had warmly invited him to their palatial residence, for lunch. The women of the house had affectionately fed him home cooked food. The grandchildren of the house were presented to him to pay their respect. On their way back, Saran and Ajay Singh were taken to the factory. When Saran realised the material produced contained much more polyester than the stamped percentage, he rejected the whole lot. It was a tough decision. The owners were shocked. It was a question of a lot of money. All that material could not be sold as the higher grade. It would cut into their profit. The Agarwala brothers were visibly perturbed. They tried convincing Saran. He was firm. He did not approve that the poorest of the poor should pay more for his day-to-day wear, like uniforms, kid's clothes, blouses, shirts sarees etc. Some nasty vibes were felt between the two parties. When Saran and Ajay Singh were about to leave the owners handed over a small brown envelope to Ajay Singh. They told him that it was the papers of the permission. "Would Mr. Saran, please look at them and reconsider passing the lot?" Saran had noticed many times these papers and a brown packet being handed over to Ajay Singh on their visits before.

On the way back to the office, Ajay Singh opened the brown envelope. To Saran's surprise, it contained a wad of Rs 500/- notes. Saran was confused. Ajay Singh also appeared to be surprised. It must have been a bundle of 100 notes. Saran did a quick calculation. Fifty thousand rupees! Oh my! He had never handled so much cash at a time. His first reaction was to tell Ajay Singh to go and return the money. Saran was angry, as well as afraid. Ajay Singh refused to go back. He said, "these notes now have my fingerprints, sir, they will have enforcement people waiting for me to prove that I have taken a bribe. I cannot return this money. Best would be to keep quiet. and not talk about it. Sir you keep it all. I promise not to mention this to anyone." Saran felt cornered. He could neither keep the money nor return it. Feeling trapped, a sort of unease settled upon him. However, before reaching office, they decided to share the money, and concluded that Ajay Singh should keep 40% and Saran should take 60%

percent share. Just before they parted, Ajay Singh warned Saran not to deposit this money in any bank, but to spend on daily expenses only.

Saran was a young sincere officer. He was keen on doing an honest job. He did not like the idea of taking bribes. Ajay Singh on the other hand was on the verge of retirement. He had been working in the Delhi office for many years and was well entrenched into the system. All his contacts were lined up. All those clients who needed their stocks to be passed would fix up with Ajay Singh to pass their stock at lower taxes in exchange for a hefty bribe.

Once Saran and Ajay Singh were travelling together after a similar inspection round. Saran asked Ajay Singh, "why do you take these brown envelopes? Why can't we just do our duty and be happy with our salaries?" Ajay Singh explained that he had a daughter, and that he was collecting money for her dowry. "The only way I can find a good alliance for my daughter is by offering a hefty dowry."

Soon Ajay Singh's daughter was married. The wedding was an extravagant affair. He was very happy, "Sir, son-in- law is in a very pivotal position in the purchase department. Daughter will be quite well-off." He informed Saran.

Within a year of the marriage Saran heard very disturbing news. Ajay Singh's married daughter had died by committing suicide. Saran rushed to Ajay Singh's house. The whole family was shaken up and grieving. "Sir, her in-laws' demands had no bounds. Besides the big wedding, and all the gold and a hefty sum, they were now demanding a car and then a bungalow. My poor child knew there would be no end to this, so she ended her life" lamented Ajay Singh.

Deeply affected by the tragedy, Saran came home, collected all the brown envelopes lying in his house and donated them to a girls' orphanage anonymously. He had 2 daughters himself, but education was the only thing he would give them in dowry. He was determined.

THREE

Two Colleagues

Amar and Sudeep worked for an economic publication called "The Business Report." Both were well-educated, efficient, and dynamic. Recently, they were selected to work on a new assignment. "The Business Report" had created a questionnaire to understand the direction of the current economic scenario. They were tasked with identifying notable personalities in the field and interviewing them to gather their perspectives. The interviews were published as "The Business Forecast." Readers eagerly looked forward to the predictions in this upcoming article. They followed it to make market decisions.

Both were skilled at their job, and they continually raised the bar by interviewing senior figures. They set a benchmark so high that even they struggled to maintain it. However, 'The Business Forecast' performed well, and the market eagerly awaited their upcoming interviews.

Amar and Sudeep had different approaches to their work. Sudeep attended high-profile events, networking with the rich and famous. He had partnered with the guest relations executive of a top hotel to secure invitations to business meetings, seminars, product launches, and high-profile conferences. Sudeep made the most of these invitations, targeting specific audiences, interacting with key individuals, and impressing them with his accent, style, and name-dropping. If necessary, he hosted parties at upscale locations, thereby expanding his network and gaining access to influential people. Thus, Sudeep contributed effectively when he was away from his desk. Overall, he did manage to rope in prominent individuals for "The Business Forecast" questionnaire.

Amar took a completely different approach. He believed in focusing on work while in the office and enjoying leisure time at home. He preferred quiet evenings with his children and avoided attending parties whenever possible. Despite his low-profile lifestyle, Amar was intelligent, efficient, and highly ambitious. He dedicated a significant amount of time to research on market movements, competition, influential figures, and the flow of money. He kept tabs on those who formulated strategies, such as government officials and politicians, as well as those who executed them, such as businessmen and corporate organizations.

Amar was determined not to be overshadowed by Sudeep's glamorous approach. He maintained a useful email list of illustrious personalities who could assist "The Business Report" in various ways. His well-researched, informative, and timely articles benefited many. Despite his low profile, Amar gained the respect of prominent businessmen for his sincerity, integrity, and market knowledge.

To illustrate, if a high-profile businessman had a problem, he might confide in Sudeep at a bar and share his concerns over a drink. However, when seeking advice on how to address the issue, he would turn to Amar.

There was intense competition between Amar and Sudeep to secure an interview with the next candidate for the "Business Forecast." Until now, they had successfully enlisted important individuals to respond to the questionnaire alternately. However, they had both reached a deadlock, with just one month left to identify the next interviewee - someone high-profile, influential in business, responsible for significant financial outflows, and capable of contributing to forecasting the future of business.

Amar delved into studying the latest trends at his desk, He sifted through financial newspapers, spotting a multinational company named "Hutch" extensively advertising telecommunication, mobile, and internet services. Recognizing the potential, Amar found out more about Hutch and its marketing head, Vicky Malhotra, who had recently relocated from New York to establish the business. Amar was excited about his discovery.

He quickly sent an email to Mr. Malhotra explaining how the interview would benefit the Hutch business and reach out to maximum potential clients. He gave a comprehensive analysis of the telecom industry showcasing his well-researched approach and deep knowledge of the market.

Meanwhile, Sudeep explored his contacts and found that,

'Hutch' had recently launched a new company. He secured an invitation to a 'product launch' hosted by Mr. Vicky Malhotra, the head of the region and met him. Sudeep pitched the idea of an interview for "The Business Forecast," and Mr. Malhotra agreed and provided his business card. "Just call up and fix an appointment," Sudeep was on cloud nine

The next day, Sudeep triumphantly announced that he had secured the next month's candidate for the 'Business Forecast.' questionnaire.

"I met Mr. Malhotra from Hutch, and he would be happy to give the interview. I am supposed to meet him this week" said Sudeep, waving the visiting card. Both Amar and Sudeep had hit upon the same candidate, but Amar was disappointed. He was almost there, had already sent an email, but he did not yet have the confirmation. while Sudeep had it. What a slip, between the cup and the lip. He decided to wait for the confirmation. Both were a team, and they should not step on each other's toes. They were anyway pursuing the same end-result.

Meanwhile Mr. Malhotra did a close check on both Sudeep and Amar. He knew Sudeep only by face value, but felt that Amar had his fingers on the pulse of the market. Mr. Malhotra chose to give the interview to Amar, based on his email.

When the day of the interview arrived, 'The Business Forecast' featured Amar's insightful conversation with Vicky Malhotra. The readers were treated to a comprehensive analysis of the telecom industry's future, showcasing Amar's dedication and market knowledge and brilliantly projecting Hutch's future.

In the end, Amar's commitment and research prevailed over Sudeep's glamorous approach. 'The Business Report' thrived, and Amar's reputation for sincerity, integrity, and market expertise solidified.

A valuable lesson was learnt through this experience. Substance triumphs over style, and true success comes to those who work diligently and intelligently in pursuit of their goals."

FOUR

Settling down

Mr Ketkar was a senior government officer working from his hometown. One day he received news that he was being transferred to Mumbai for a new assignment. Excitement and nervousness mingled within him as he prepared to move to the dynamic city.

Fortunately, his predecessor's flat was already assigned to him and Mr. Ketkar was scheduled to stay at Rajdeep Mahal on Marine Drive in Bombay. However, for the initial 8 days, Ketkar could reside at the government guest house. Upon his arrival at Bombay by train, he was pleasantly surprised when Mr. Patel appeared at the station to pick him up. Ketkar had not anticipated anyone's presence, but he was delighted when Patel introduced himself as his assistant and offered to help him in settling down. Together, they headed towards the government guest house.

To Ketkar's dismay, the guest house turned out to be quite unpleasant. It lacked the convenience of running hot water. Whenever he desired to take a bath, he had to request the cook to heat a half-filled bucket of water in the kitchen. Even the morning tea was served after a considerable wait. Although the kitchen possessed a gas cylinder, the cook used it sparingly due to its scarcity and the 20-day waiting period for replacement.

Furthermore, Patel had cautioned Ketkar not to trust anyone, emphasizing that everyone was needy. Ketkar, thinking that it was only a temporary situation for a week, resolved to manage it. However, he became more cautious about securing his minimal possessions and cash each time he left the guest house.

On joining on Monday, Patel was there in office to welcome him and show him to his cabin. Patel introduced him to the staff and clients explaining the prevailing systems. Ketkar asked to meet his predecessor, but Patel informed that he was on leave, and would be going away from Bombay only at the month end after his children finished their final exams. Ketkar was disappointed, but expected to continue staying at the guest house, till he could move into his allotted house.

On Friday evening, Ketkar was informed by the cook that Collector Saheb and two of his officers were scheduled to arrive on Monday. Consequently, all the rooms in the guest house needed to be vacated for their use. Frustrated, Ketkar asked, "Where am I supposed to go?" However, nobody knew the answer, as the cook simply followed instructions. Ketkar's only thought was Patel. He knew that Patel was a reliable person who could potentially provide a solution. Despite Ketkar's experience as a seasoned officer, adjusting to this new environment in office and the city, seemed like a daunting task. Over the past five days, Patel had taken good care of Ketkar and introduced him to the new job environment. Ketkar silently thanked Patel and realized the importance of having someone like him to establish his own position.

On Saturday morning, Patel had invited Ketkar for lunch, and during this meal, Ketkar planned to seek Patel's assistance in finding alternative accommodation. The problem of finding a place to stay weighed heavily on Ketkar's mind, so he arrived early at Patel's place and explained his predicament. Together, they embarked on a search for a hotel. However, securing a hotel room through the government system proved to be challenging. Approval had to be obtained beforehand, and reimbursements for expenses would only be received after a minimum of three months. Ketkar did not possess sufficient funds to cover these costs, and he began to worry about how things would unfold. They visited three of the most affordable hotels near the office, but none had any available accommodations. The hotels informed them that bookings had to be made at least a month in advance in Bombay. Ketkar's anxiety grew steadily.

Disappointed, the two men returned to Patel's residence. Upon entering, Ketkar had his first encounter with Guni, Patel's little daughter. Despite her shyness, she had an infectious smile and boundless curiosity. Peeking out from behind her mother at first, she soon came up and provided Ketkar with a jug of water to wash his hands, as their entire building lacked running water. She arranged stainless-steel plates, bowls, glasses, and drinking water for their lunch. The house exuded simplicity, cleanliness, and a pleasant aroma of freshly prepared Indian cuisine.

Both men, famished from their search for a hotel, settled down for lunch. Patel's elder son joined them at the table. Guni graciously served all three of them a meal consisting of dal, rice, two types of sabjis, kachumber, kheer, and piping hot chapatis that her mother was preparing in the kitchen. This was Ketkar's first experience of a delicious, home-cooked meal in Bombay, which he thoroughly enjoyed. The three of them ate in silence, satiated by the sumptuous lunch. Guni entered briefly to offer *supari,* after which both she and her mother sat down for their own lunch in the kitchen.

Afterward, they gathered in the living room, resuming their discussion on where Ketkar should reside starting from the following day. Ketkar was visibly worried about his stay in Mumbai and how he would cope with his lack of accommodation. With a touch of courage, Patel spoke up, "Saheb, please pardon me, but may I make a suggestion? I leave for the office at 8:30 AM and return by 7:30 PM. It is only a matter of dinner and overnight rest. You are welcome to stay here with us." Normally, Ketkar was too proud to stay even with relatives. However, circumstances had forced him to a corner. He was uncertain whether his finances would last until his next paycheck. Additionally, being new to his office and the city of Bombay, he was unsure if his office would approve the extra expenses. Ideally, he should have stayed with his predecessor, who was living in the house that was now allotted to Ketkar. Unfortunately, his children had exams and his family was in the process of moving out of their current residence. Ultimately, Ketkar had no choice but to accept Patel's invitation.

On Monday morning, Ketkar packed his belongings at the guest house and headed to the office with his luggage. After work, he intended to go directly to Patel's place. Ketkar felt anxious, but Patel reassured him and expressed eagerness to have his boss as a houseguest. In the evening, when they arrived at Patel's house, they were greeted by Guni. She noticed Mr. Ketkar's hesitation. Determined to make him feel at home, she promptly took his briefcase and placed it in the specially prepared room for him. Returning with a jug of water, she offered it to Mr. Ketkar for him to freshen up. Her demeanour implied that Mr. Ketkar was a regular visitor to their home, making him feel at ease. Once he had finished washing up and emerged from the room, she handed him the newspaper while dinner was being laid.

"Is dinner ready?" Patel enquired; a bit concerned. "Certainly! Today is a special day because we have a distinguished guest. I have specially prepared Kachumber for Ketkar kaka," she playfully teased her father, and smiled affectionately at Mr. Ketkar.

Guni, with her innocent yet perceptive eyes, sensed that Mr. Ketkar needed help settling into their home. She took it upon herself to be his guide. Amid unfamiliar surroundings, a young and inexperienced girl emanated an aura of comfort and joviality that put Ketkar, an elderly man, at ease. Every evening, she served dinner, and as Ketkar retired to freshen up, she would stealthily slip into his room and neatly make his bed. Rising early each morning, she would eagerly bring him tea and enthusiastically announce the day's breakfast menu. Her exuberance and playful nature infused the entire household with joy and liveliness. She effortlessly interacted, teased, assisted, served, joked, and conversed with each member of the household individually. It seemed that a strong bond, aptly named "Guni," connected every member of the household. If her brother desired a cricket bat, it was Guni who relayed the message to their father. If her mother needed money for purchasing vegetables, it was Guni who fearlessly approached her father's wallet. When her father yearned for a snack, he would entrust Guni with the task of conveying his request to her mother, emphasizing that it would be delightful if she could prepare it for Mr. Ketkar. Even before he could voice his needs, Guni intuitively sensed Mr. Ketkar's requirements. As the days passed, Guni not only made Ketkar feel like a true member of this humble yet contented family, but also an integral part of Mumbai. She guided him to the grocer and the chemist shops when he needed to buy, showed him the park where he could go for a walk, the place where he could get a bus or taxi, and introduced him to the neighbours whenever they came across one. Ketkar's affection for this young girl grew, akin to that of a doting father for his own daughter.

Within a few days Ketkar became comfortable in Patel's house, and was familiar with all the members of the family. He even gave their son maths lessons in the evening, showed some card tricks to Guni, and shared stories and experiences from his previous office with Patel.

Suddenly, Ketkar got a letter saying that he could move into the new house that was allotted to him. Ketkar was to move immediately. Instead of being happy to get the news, Ketkar felt a lump in his throat. Leaving the affectionate Patel family was not going to be easy. They all looked sad as well. Patel had truly helped Ketkar to settle down in Mumbai.

FIVE

Sheema and the Birds

"Huu Chiu Chiu chewy chu," chirped the two sparrows that had entered Sheema's house and were looking for a place to nest. Every year, they made a nest in the beautiful chandelier hanging from the ceiling, finding it a perfect place to lay their eggs and hatch them. Sheema would be very excited when the 'he' and 'she' sparrow kept flying in with blades of grass, strings, twigs, and sticks from the broom, making quite a noise. Their excitement in preparing for the new arrivals in their family was contagious. Sheema knew the routine by heart.

Her mother would come and shoo the sparrow couple away, but the little birds would not listen. Then she would instruct the sweeper to remove the nest and all the twigs that had fallen on the carpet, right below the chandelier. The maid would clear the carpet but would never be able to reach the nest, saying, "Too high." So, the sparrows were allowed to nest until they had laid their eggs, and the nestlings flew away. Sheema watched their progress with curiosity. Various noises came from the nest. The initial tweets and excitement were replaced by silence while the eggs were hatching. Then, you would hear a teeny-weeny *chu chun*. After a day or two, another *chu chun*. And then, again, the excitement of the sparrow couple flying in and out of the window, this time with tiny morsels of food, not twigs.

Soon, the little birds would also learn to fly, and Sheema would wait to catch a glimpse of the little ones flying off. Within a month or so, the nest would be abandoned, and its remnants would stay there until the Diwali spring cleaning took place. Just before Diwali, her mother would get hold of a labourer to come with a high ladder, clean the chandelier, wipe the Belgian glass prisms, change the bulbs, and, of course, remove the abandoned nest.

&&&&

"Every week on Wednesdays and Saturdays, the fish vendor would call out, and Mother would be waiting for him to buy some fresh fish. He brought a variety of fish. Sometimes it was Bombil and Bangda, and on Saturdays, he carried prawns or crabs, pomfret, or *Surmai*. Sheema watched as her mother and the fisherman haggled on the prices and then sat in the veranda to clean the fish. The prawns were peeled, and the fish cut into fillets, slices, or cubes. The crabs were always brought live, and it was a circus to remove their shells, and get them ready for cooking.

During this activity, a few crows would gather for their share of the fish. Their cawing and attempts to shoo each other away created a lively scene until a bold crow would swoop in, grab a piece, and fly away. Sheema watched all this with glee and thought, 'Both the crow and sparrow are birds, but so different from each other.'"

&&&&

One of Sheema's neighbours had a pet parrot kept in a cage. Sheema and her friends often went to their house to listen to the parrot. They called the neighbour "Parrot Uncle." He would get the parrot to whistle and say a few words. How melodious it sounded! The parrot repeated 'mummy' and said 'hello hello' and called one of the children by his name. How fascinating this bird was, with its bright green colour, the black ring around its neck, the red beak, and its whistle, leaving Sheema in awe. That day, Sheema decided she was going to learn to whistle. She rounded her lips, rolled her tongue, and kept practicing. She asked Parrot Uncle what the bird ate. "My Mithu loves green chillies, soaked Channa dal, and guavas." Sheema went home and asked her mom to give her all these things to eat so that she could start whistling.

&&&

Occasionally, a flock of Mynas would come to the tree outside the house and make sweet noises, as if a conversation were being sung. Their melodious voices enticed Sheema to go to the window and look out for them. They were quick and graceful black birds with nimble yellow feet and yellow beaks.

On the parapet of the house opposite, a whole lot of pigeons sat. Sheema did not like the pigeons very much. They just sat still for hours and made a muffled sort of noise, as if they had a stuffy nose.

In the months of May and June came the sweet cooing of the Cuckoo. The cuckoo would announce the onset of summer with its sweet coo hoo. Sheema had learned that if she also made the same sound, the cuckoo considered her to be stiff competition and would coo even louder. How she enjoyed instigating the Cuckoo. It was as if the bird was talking to her and saying, "I am better and louder than you." Sheema wondered what made the cuckoo's voice so rich. Was it the summer heat that cleared its throat, or the sweetness of the mangoes, or the freshness brought by the April showers?

&&&

One day Sheema went out on the terrace to play. No one had been on the terrace for a long time. While she was running around, she saw a large kite circling in the sky. She watched the kite. It circled twice, then sat on a wire running across. Again, it flew off, circled a few times, and disappeared into a tree. Sheema continued playing on the terrace. Suddenly, she felt a sharp pull on her head and saw the large bird flying away. The kite made a very typical noise as it went by, "cheeeeee–eeeeeee-eeennnnnnee." Sheema thought the bird wanted to play with her. She was very excited. She went down and told her mother how a kite tried to pull her hair. Her mother told her that the kite was not trying to play with her; it was trying to grab her with its claws, as they do with their prey. "But I am so much larger than the bird; surely, it knows it can't pick me up?" asked Sheema. Mother said, "The kite must have a nest somewhere close by, probably on our terrace itself. When you went there, it felt threatened. So, it was warning you not to harm its little ones." Sheema decided she should not go on the terrace and disturb any nest; she wanted many more kites to fly in the sky.

*****

One Sunday morning, Sheema and her father went for a walk in the park. He mentioned having spotted some peacocks there, so if they were lucky, they might get to see them too. Sheema was very excited, having seen pictures of peacocks in her book. The images portrayed the bird with a long and colourful tail, though she thought the book may have painted it too brightly. "Surely, no bird can have such an inky blue colour," she thought.

As they strolled in the park on a bright sunny morning, the air felt cool and fresh on her cheeks. She danced and pranced about on the grass, but there was no sign of the peacocks. Walking further inside the park with her father, they still saw no sign. Eventually, they decided to walk back home. Sheema was a bit disappointed, but just as they approached the exit gate, her father pressed her hand and whispered, "Look." Right in front of them, perched on the pillar of the gate, was the most magnificent bird she had ever seen in her whole life. Its colour was even brighter than any picture she had seen, and it had a sheen on its dark blue body. The tail, flowing down the pillar, seemed to be embroidered from the finest threads, more beautiful than any evening gown she had seen on TV. Just then, a few peahens flew to the open ground on the right, and "lo and behold," two peacocks were dancing with their tails spread out, while the peahens grazed around them. "What a sight!" thought Sheema. Even her father exclaimed, "Ah ha," when he saw the dancing peacocks.

That was the day, Sheema thanked God for bringing her to this earth and showing her such beautiful creatures. She felt like hugging life itself.

SIX
Merry Mumbai

Veena's husband had recently been transferred to Mumbai, bringing her immense joy upon hearing the news. She believed that Mumbai offered ample opportunities for those aspiring to achieve something meaningful. Having completed the phases of marriage and raising two children, Veena was eager to re-enter the professional sphere. Six years ago, she made the sacrifice of leaving her promising career to prioritize her personal life. The decision led her to marriage, relocation to Delhi, and dedicating herself to her husband and their two children.

Now, with the prospect of a fresh start in Mumbai, both Veena and her husband agreed that it was time for her to resume her career. Veena was well-acquainted with Mumbai, having previously worked in a travel agency and undertaken a post-graduation placement with a renowned publication in the city. Although she could have returned to that publication, she needed a job with flexible hours due to her motherly responsibilities.

Motivated by the London Planner, Veena envisioned starting a similar travel magazine in Mumbai. Her mind teemed with ideas for the magazine's content—ranging from iconic landmarks like the Prince of Wales Museum and Mani Bhavan to art galleries, Marathi theatre, literary clubs, Max Mueller Bhavan, historical buildings with period architecture. She planned to cover the diverse communities of Mumbai, including the Parsis, Kolis, migrants, business communities, the dabbawallas, and residents of Hindu colony. She also planned to cover music appreciation programs, the Isckon temple, and the ever-fascinating world of Bollywood. With enthusiasm and a wealth of ideas, Veena was poised to embark on this exciting new chapter in her professional journey.

From her previous experiences, Veena had acquired knowledge in printing, including skills in Adobe Photoshop, offset printing, title verification, and journal registration. The first crucial step in her new venture was to choose a fitting name for her publication. After careful consideration, she settled on the title "Merry Mumbai," which translated to "Meri Mumbai" or "My Mumbai" in Hindi. The next task on her agenda was to officially register the title to obtain permission for publishing her magazine.

Upon settling in Mumbai, Veena selected a working day to visit the court for the registration process. Despite uncertainties about the duration, she had arranged for the baby's care and managed household chores to ensure her absence would not be felt. Departing after the family's lunch, she embarked on a long drive to the court, anticipating potential delays due to traffic.

Upon reaching the court's entrance gate, Veena found herself surrounded by a group of aggressive lawyers seeking business opportunities. They were vying for some business from her in desperation. Most of them were in the age-group of 30 to 50 years and looked educated. To be a lawyer, one had to have at least a post graduate degree. After all that, if they had to run after clients for small legal assignments, Veena felt more than sorry for their state. Amongst them, one youngish man and a middle-aged woman caught her attention. That man must be having a family to support. Although he was wearing a white shirt and a black tie, he seemed to be in dire financial need. He was almost begging her to give him the job. But he was pushed away by the older woman, who seemed to need a legal assignment just to earn her two meals a day.

"Excuse me," Veena ventured, her voice tinged with confusion. "I am here to register my publication, 'Merry Mumbai.' Can you help me with the process?"

Once they understood the purpose of her visit, their interest waned. Veena hesitated, feeling anxious. "I need to know where to get the registration form and how to proceed," she explained, trying to keep her voice steady.

The lawyer shrugged nonchalantly. "You'll find the forms at the government counter. Fill it out and get it stamped," he replied, already turning his attention back to see if anyone else was looking out for a lawyer.

She procured the relevant one-page form, for Rs 25/- which required filling and submission at the government counter for stamping. Locating the stamping counter proved to be a challenge in the somewhat dilapidated building, which, despite its majestic exterior, was poorly maintained inside. The air was thick with the scent of dust and paper, and the din of voices echoed off the walls, adding to her disorientation. Navigating through numerous corridors and seeking directions along the way, she eventually found a small window with a long, slow-moving queue outside. After what felt like an hour, her turn arrived, and the form was successfully stamped.

Inquiring at the counter about the next steps, Veena learned that the contents of the form needed to be transcribed onto a stamp paper and notarized. Upon exiting, Veena noticed that the swarm of lawyers had shifted their attention to another individual. Undeterred, she approached them to inquire about obtaining a stamp paper. Now, however, they seemed too preoccupied to assist her. Determined, she cornered one of them who gestured towards an office deep inside the building where stamp papers were supposedly available. Rushing through the labyrinth of dingy corridors, she finally located the window, where stamp papers were sold. she discovered no queue and breathed a sigh of relief. Glancing at her watch, it seemed like her task might be completed that day.

Taking money from her purse, Veena approached the cashier as if purchasing a train ticket. However, to her dismay, the cashier casually informed her that they had run out of stamp papers. This revelation came as a rude shock, and worry filled her mind at the thought of having to return another day. Who would take care of her child at home? While contemplating this, she asked, "What time should I come tomorrow?" The response was uncertain, "Not sure if the stock would be there." Nonplussed, she cursed the government for its apparent callousness. Wouldn't the entire legal machinery come to a standstill without stamp papers? She thought.

Disheartened by the lack of assistance, Veena forced a smile and murmured her thanks before moving away from the government counter. With each step, her patience was tested, replaced by a growing sense of frustration at the bureaucratic hurdles she faced throughout.

She wandered aimlessly within the building, asking anyone she encountered if they had a stamp paper to sell. Determined to complete her task that day, she returned to the lawyers, who were now scattered—some seated under a tree, others seeking new clients, and some working with a typewriter to secure typing assignments at least. Veena couldn't help but question the efficiency of the judiciary system. After 40 years of independence, it seemed disorganized, and struggled to provide even two meals a day to its lawyers. This was particularly frustrating considering the backlog of legal cases pending for 10 to 15 years, with some extending into the next generation. Realizing that it would be another month before she could return to the court, Veena hung around, contemplating the challenges of navigating the legal system.

It was nearly 5:30 PM, with everything scheduled to close by 6 PM. Veena's eyes darted in desperation as she stood alone, unsure of where to go or how to proceed. Three lawyers were wrapping up their day and heading home. One of them, glancing at her, muttered as he passed by, "You wanted a stamp paper, right? Ask that guy across the road; he might be able to help you." Without hesitation, she ran across the road, keeping her eyes on the man. As she dashed, narrowly avoiding a passing car, her heart pounding in her chest., her sole focus was on obtaining the stamp paper that day. "Excuse me," she called out breathlessly, her voice tinged with desperation. "I need your help."

The man, dressed in a black coat like a lawyer, seemed well-off and not in pursuit of clients. Catching up with him, Veena urgently explained her need for a stamp paper, and he instructed her to wait. She handed him Rs 250, and he walked away towards the street with her money. Watching him closely, she saw him attempt to cross the road just as the traffic lights turned green. Realizing that he may vanish with her money, she ran behind him, crossed the road amidst traffic, and followed him to a somewhat disreputable tea stall.

There, he engaged with a teenage boy, handed him her money, and made gestures. The boy disappeared into a dark kitchen and returned with a rolled paper. The lawyer, turning around, found Veena standing behind him. Annoyed, he scolded her for not waiting as instructed. Confused by his reaction, she hastily took the stamp paper and walked away, pondering why he had snapped at her.

Returning to the court, she encountered a crowd pouring out from everywhere. It was a lengthy walk to where the typists were stationed, most of whom had finished their work. Finding one typist still occupied with a client, Veena approached him. The typist indicated three more pages he needed to type and said she could wait. Despite realizing it would take an hour for the three pages, Veena acknowledged the limited choices. As she waited in line, her mind raced with thoughts of her family waiting at home and the mounting pressure to achieve maximum on that day itself. Grateful she was not tending to her baby, she contemplated how her outings would have been constrained if she had to return home within three hours to attend to her baby's needs.

As Veena waited for the typist to complete his work, time seemed to crawl at a snail's pace. Court employees poured out, and the street traffic increased, accompanied by heightened honking. A few women employees in sarees paused for tea and 'pakoras' before heading home. Some male colleagues joined them, engaging in jokes and flirtation. For the women, the challenges of the day were far from over—they would embark on a journey to Churchgate station, endure a crowded local train ride for at least an hour, navigate bustling streets to pick up groceries, and upon reaching home, dive into the tasks of preparing dinner, packing lunch for the next day, attending to their children, and ensuring they had enough rest.

"Madam, give me your content," the typist said, having finished the three-page assignment. He stretched, inserted a fresh paper along with her stamp paper, and she sighed with relief. This typist was the only one who had not caused her any trouble, only making her wait. At least he was willing to complete her task at this late hour without complaints. She handed over the form, and he took only 15 minutes to type on the stamp paper. Grateful for his assistance, she asked him about the next steps. "You will have to notarize these papers, submit them, get a receipt, and wait. Typically, it takes between 15 days to 3 months for the court to respond. They will send you a letter instructing you on what to do next." Thanking him, she paid up and walked toward her car.

Exhausted and with no energy left for additional tasks, she decided to find a notary near her house and return to submit her application later. Throwing the papers onto the seat next to her, she began driving home. The car's AC provided some solace, but she soon encountered peak-hour traffic, having to wait at traffic signals every two minutes.

Throughout her day's journey, Veena's emotions fluctuated between hope and despair, determination, and doubt. But she persevered, driven by a steadfast belief in her ability to overcome any obstacle.

Arriving home completely fatigued, but satisfied with having achieved at least something, she walked into her house at 8:15 PM. A heavy silence hung in the air. She had left at 1 PM and returned after 8 hours with only one typed paper, but she was not inclined to explain. Safely stashing the papers in a drawer, she focused on preparing dinner.

A few months later, a major scam was exposed, revealing Abdul Telgi as the mastermind who had defrauded the government of crores of rupees by distributing counterfeit stamp papers through unauthorized channels. Telgi orchestrated the scheme by deliberately causing a shortage of legitimate stamp papers and then flooding the market with fake ones through illicit means. The legal case against him brought to light the various corrupt methods employed by Telgi in the printing and distribution of fraudulent stamp papers.

Veena had firsthand experience of the hardships faced by ordinary citizens to get hold of a stamp paper. How the public suffered, when someone in power amassed wealth in millions by exploiting millions of people.

So, within the labyrinths of what seemed like a "Merry Mumbai" there was a dark side to it too. Something more for Veena to cover in her magazine.

SEVEN

New friends

Mr. Joshi was posted to Bombay, but his children continued their schooling in the hometown. It was decided that his family would visit him during holidays once their father settles down. Joshi's family was eagerly waiting to go to Bombay to spend Diwali vacation with their father. The train tickets were booked the day the children's holidays began.

His daughter Zaee was in college. She longed to shop on the streets of Bombay. Zaee had already found out from her friends, that she should go to Linking Road in Bombay to pick up tops, chappals, sandals, purses, hairpins, clips, nighties, gowns, dress material.... everything that a college girl would want. She was very excited. Joshi's wife was looking forward to the 'high life.' She planned to visit her relatives and show off her husband's position. First time in her married life, Mrs. Joshi was proud of her husband. After all, he had a spacious flat on Marine drive. All her relatives lived in Dadar, Santacruz, Thane etc. Not so upmarket and so far away from downtown, she thought. His son Yash had already boasted to all his friends, how he was going to Bombay to see all the fancy cars and go to *Chowpatty.*

Joshi went to pick up his family at the station. On their arrival, there was a lot of excitement in Yash's voice. Zaee tried to hold hers, but could not hide her curiosity. On the station itself, her eyes were scouring for Bollywood actresses, and women wearing tight slacks and perfume and latest fashions. Mrs. Joshi felt a bit shy of her husband, as this was the first time they had stayed away from each other for so long. Joshi called a coolie to pick up the luggage. The children picked up their own bags. Halfway down the platform, Mrs. Joshi remembered that they had not fixed the charges with the coolie. "Now he will charge us double, and we will have to pay!" Mr. Joshi grunted. On streaming out of the railway station, Joshi led his family to the private car parking. A large car with a smart driver awaited them. Both the children gasped. A car? Daddy, have you bought a car? Is this for us? Joshi shushed them and asked the driver to load the suitcases in the trunk of the car. As they got in, Joshi told them, that one of the factory owners had offered the car to pick them up. What a nice guy he must be, thought his family. As the car rolled smoothly across Flora fountain, Churchgate, Nariman point, Marine drive, his family's eyes popped out, each had a smile of awe on their face, and no words would come out. Zaee and Yash exchanged wide eyed glances, and nodded at each other. They knew, they were in for a good time.

On reaching home, Mrs Joshi took out all the snacks she had made at home, but would not let the children eat back home, as it was made for 'Diwali in Bombay'. The whole family approved of the house. It was clean, big and Dad seemed to be well organised. They had tea, and *'Shev, chakli, Mathia and kanola'* and sat, chatted, and caught up with all the stories each one had to tell. Mrs Joshi seemed to laugh extra loudly at every word, Zaee suddenly put on airs as if she were a model, Yash could not help expressing joy and wonder at everything he saw.

Zaee and Yash got up the next morning to strange noises. A woman in a printed saree was making 'chapatis'. She was the efficient Bombay maid who came in before Mr. Joshi left for office and made *chapati-bhaji* for his 'dabba' which he carried along with him. There were car horns blowing. The salty, humid smell of the sea, mingled with the rhythmic beating of the waves. Yash ran out in the balcony to see a river of cars flowing towards town. Cars of all colours, but in 3 shapes predominantly. The Ambassador, the Fiat, and the Standard occasionally. Yash got busy watching the lively scene, the odd imported car, the well-dressed men sitting in them, and the young executives walking across on the foot paths, and started dreaming that one day he would also go to office in this style with a brief-case in hand. He was so absorbed in his own thoughts, that he did not notice Zaee when she came and stood behind him. She said, "Stop staring at the road, Yash. 'See the sea'." Yash raised his head and looked beyond the horizon. The tide was just coming in. One could see the white froth of the waves as they approached the shoreline. The sky was blue, the air was cool and crisp, the sun was shining bright, and occasionally, a flock of parrots screeched from one tree to another. Both the children stood in the balcony and absorbed the smell of the sea and the sound of the horns for a long time. Yash said, 'See the sea,' sounds like 'C the C.' Zaee looked at him perplexed. He smiled and explained 'be a bee' or 'B a B.'

Zaee understood and said' Q in the Q, Jay is J, Tee off at tea," and Yash added 'pee on a pea' and both laughed.

While the children were in the balcony, Mr. Joshi gave Mrs. Joshi a lot of information. " Tomorrow, you can go to Crawford market to pick up some vegetable, fish, meat, etc. during the day. If you need money please take 200 rupees out of the envelope in the grey suitcase on top of the cupboard. The maid comes only in the morning for one hour. She will make chapatis for all of us, clean the house, and the bathrooms. If you need any groceries, there is a shop on the corner. My diary in the drawer has the phone numbers of all the relatives, you can take the children for a walk on Marine drive after 4 O' clock when the heat reduces a bit, and I will be back only around seven.

****

Mr. Patil was Joshi's colleague in office. On the weekend the Joshi family met the Patils. Mr. Patil offered to arrange a car and driver for the Joshis to visit all their relatives. Mrs. Patil gave them a lot of info, on where Yash could go to play cricket in the mornings, where they would get to see the Bollywood actors, where film shootings took place, what to do at the Gateway of India, where to eat near the Taj hotel etc. The Joshis were fascinated with all the possibilities Mumbai had to offer.

Little Vasudha, Patil's daughter, fell in love with Zaee tai. She was so good-looking, spoke so well, was so affectionate, and what a lovely Punjabi dress she wore. It was white cotton, with red Jaipuri motifs on it. The churidar was plain white, the kurta had large motifs in red vegetable dye, and the chunni had the same motifs but in a smaller size. She wore a light lipstick, had a flawless, fair complexion and a smile on her face. Vasudha loved her straight, soft silky hair, as compared to her dry rough curly locks, which once tangled would have to be cut off, as there was no comb or brush which could sort them out.

Vasudha was chattering away and telling the Joshis a lot of stories of the people around and her life in general. She also showed Zaee tai a dress material that her uncle Ajumama had given her for her birthday. She wanted to wear it quickly, but "Mummy is just not giving it for stitching". "I will find a good tailor, but you know how they are! Not one will stitch well, charge a lot, and take so much time to deliver," said Mrs Patil. On hearing this, both Mrs. Joshi and Zaee said, " Do not worry about the tailors. We can stitch it for Vasudha." Vasudha was thrilled to hear that she could wear a new frock soon. Next day it was decided that Vasudha will go to the Joshis, in the afternoon, and Zaee will take her measurement, and decide on the pattern, cut the material, and make it ready for stitching. Then one day they can come to the Patil's place to use the sewing machine and stitch up the frock. Vasudha was jumping with joy at the thought of her new dress, and that Zaee tai was going to stitch it for her.

Next day, as promised, Vasudha and her brother set off to Joshi's place after lunch with her dress material. While Zaee tai cut the cloth and made it ready to be stitched into a frock, the two boys went out in the compound to play cricket, and Vasudha's brother taught Yash a lot of batting techniques and bowling methods he had learnt at his cricket academy. So far Yash had just played gully cricket with his friends outside his house, and it was a revelation to him to know how much more there was to learn in cricket in terms of footwork, fielding and even in taking a catch. The main thing was to be fit and agile, and Yash was determined to work-out in the gym to increase his stamina and fitness level. Zaee tai got busy searching for a nice pattern for Vasudha's dress amid the little girl's chatter. Vasudha wanted to tell Zaee tai everything that happened in her life, about all the people in the building, her school, her friends, etc.

"You know, Kathuria's son, who lives near our house, just returned from 'foreign.' They always go abroad during vacations. He distributed imported chocolates and watches on his birthday as return gifts to all the children. Zaee tai, you see, they have money to throw around. They have big cars, and he goes for tuitions, and always drinks Coke and Fanta, and eats potato chips anytime of the day! And do you know, Zaee tai, shall I tell you a secret? My friend Suma's elder sister has a boyfriend. He works in the garage opposite our house. Every day in the evening, we go down to play in the compound. Many children come. Nowadays we play in the sand, which is deposited outside our house for the construction of the building nearby. The construction work stops by five o'clock, then, all of us go down and make castles in the sand. My friends and I have made the biggest castle. Today, in the evening, we are going to complete it. But there is a problem. There are two older boys who come to wash the cars in the building. They are eyeing our castle. Yesterday, they came to break our castle. When we told them not to break it, you know what they did? They pulled all the girls aside and started pinching our chests and saying *"Mishi mishi.'* No breaking the castles of all the girls who let us do *'mishi mishi'*

Vasudha's chatter went on. Zaee tai suddenly became alert. 'What? Something was wrong here.'

"Will those boys come again today?" she asked Vasudha.

"Yes, they do come there."

"Okay, on your way home, today I'll go with you, show me those boys."

"Yes, I will," said Vasudha absentmindedly, as she concentrated on how Zaee tai was cutting the dress material in shape.

Later, Mrs. Joshi gave the children *ladoo, chivda,* and sherbat. Zaee tai went with the Patil children to drop them home. As they neared the home, Zaee saw a big mound of sand and some children playing there.

"Are those two car washer boys there?" Zaee asked.

Vasudha pointed at them innocently. Zaee went closer to them, held one arm of each of the boys, and twisted it so badly that one of them winced. She held both the boys in dire pain, with their hands twisted, till they fell in the sand. She pinned them with her foot and asked, "What were you trying to do to these kids? What is 'mishi mishi'?" She freed one hand and before they knew it, she slapped one of them so hard, his face lost all colour, and tears started flowing from the corner of his eyes. The other one was visibly afraid. All the children gathered around them and realized that these boys had done something wrong. The boys felt so humiliated in front of all the children. "If I see you anywhere close to any child here, I am going to report you to the police." She warned the children not to play with these boys anymore. All of them nodded in affirmation. Then she left their twisted arms suddenly, and the two boys ran away.

Meanwhile, the two mothers went to Crawford market to shop. They returned with lots of fruits, vegetables, and goodies. They also bought diyas, crackers, rangoli and flowers to celebrate Diwali. Not only that, but Mrs Patil showed Mrs. Joshi around Gandhi market which had beautiful sarees, embroidered materials, household goods and latest gadgets. Both ladies enjoyed their outing.

The two families invited each other for meals, went for outings, benefited from each other's company, and felt happy about the time spent they together. Soon, the Diwali vacation came to an end, and it was time for the Joshi family to head back, carrying fond memories with them.

EIGHT

Revenge by Chance

Anita was chatting with her friend, Suma

Anita: Hey, do you remember when Chiki aunty used to visit from the States during high school? The house would be buzzing with activity.

Suma: Oh, yeah! She always brought a lot of gifts for everyone.

Anita: Yes, she is visiting us again. I am so excited. Whenever she is here, all her friends, especially Rekha and Sunil, drop by too. We have a lot of activities planned. It is a hectic time. Chiki auntie's visits bring fun times for us.

Suma: Who are Rekha and Sunil?

Anita: They were quite a story, you know? Ran away during college and got married.

Suma: No way! How did they manage?

Anita: It was not easy. No money, no place to live, and society did not spare them. Finally, one set of the parents gave them a servant quarter to live and the other set of parents paid their college fees. Took them about 4-5 years to settle down.

Suma: That's intense. Did anyone else from their group do something like that?

Anita: Nope, after seeing Rekha and Sunil's struggle, and looking at their plight, none of their friends dared to do the same. At the time, Deshmukh sir, was very fond of Chiki aunty, but shelved his feelings for Chiki. They both decided it was wise to maintain a distance.

Friend: Wow. What happened to Chiki then?

Anita: She eventually married a well-settled guy from the United States and lives there quite happily.

Sunil and Deshmukh sir were the best of friends. Sunil would arrange for outings, picnics, whenever Chiki was in town. Anita and her whole family went along with Chiki's friends. That is how Anita got to know Deshmukh sir.

Chiki was Anita's mom's younger sister. One day Chiki said she was going out for lunch. Deshmukh sir came to pick her up around 11 AM. It was a rainy day. Chiki did not return till late. Mom got worried. She called Rekha to ensure that all of them were alright. Rekha said that Sunil and she had not gone. Mom became worried. Chiki had a proper family tucked away in the States. What was she doing with Deshmukh on this rainy day? There was an awkward silence when Chiki returned late in the night. No one said anything. Anita was fond of her aunt. She wished for Chiki to have her cozy life in the States without any emotional upheavals.

Soon Anita was in the first year of college. She went in the science stream. That year the university decided that all students needed to pass a compulsory paper on 'Civics and Administration.' Anita was amused to find that Deshmukh sir was taking their classes. He was a very good teacher. She enjoyed his classes. Occasionally he would inquire about Chiki aunty.

Anita and her college friends were typical group of girls, finding amusement in poking fun at their lecturers. One day, their attention fixated on Deshmukh sir, who, to their amusement, was spotted wearing shoes without socks. The sight elicited a hearty laugh from the girls, and Anita could not resist sharing the humorous incident with her aunt, Chiki, when she visited them next.

"Chiki, you won't believe what happened! All the girls were laughing at Deshmukh sir. He looked so funny," Anita recounted to her aunt with a chuckle.

Chiki, being the mischievous soul she was, decided to pick on Deshmukh. When all their friends had gathered at Anita's home, Chiki playfully teased Deshmukh in front of their friends.

"So, you wear shoes without socks, is it? And do you put on loads of makeup for your classes? Maybe a shirt that looks like a blouse?" she added her own "*Mirch masala*" to the banter.

Deshmukh, known for his impeccable dressing, immediately sensed Anita's involvement. He took her aside, visibly agitated, and explained, "Anita, those were 'mojadies' I was wearing. They are supposed to be worn without socks."

Anita, embarrassed by the revelation, stammered, "No sir, yes sir," her face turning crimson. It was one thing to enjoy a laugh behind someone's back, but being confronted to face the consequences was an entirely different story.

A year passed, and Anita had pushed the incident to the back of her mind until one day, Deshmukh summoned her to his office.

"Anita, Mr. Deshmukh from the Arts Faculty wants to see you," she was informed.

"Okay," she replied, assuming it was something personal, perhaps a message for her aunt. However, engrossed in exam preparations, she decided to delay the visit until after the practical exams in two days and the impending final exams.

As she was about to forget about it, a second message arrived, stating that Deshmukh had visited their faculty looking for her. Despite thinking it could not be that urgent, her physics lecturer insisted she go immediately.

The Arts Faculty was a 20-minute walk away, under the scorching afternoon sun. She approached Deshmukh sir's room with a faint hope he might not be in. A "Come in" echoed from inside as she knocked on the door.

Without wasting time, Deshmukh sir informed her about a prestigious debate in town, attended by dignitaries. He had chosen her as the student participant. An impatient Anita immediately declined.

"No sir, it's not possible right now. My final exams start next week," she asserted.

"But you don't understand. Only five people are speaking – a politician, two professionals, and two students from the whole university, one boy, and one girl. You are going to be that girl," he said with excitement.

Tempting as it was, Anita knew she could not participate. She had followed her last-minute study strategy throughout the year and planned to cram for the exams in the final 15 days. Declining, she was about to leave when Deshmukh insisted.

"What's your problem? I will prepare you; I have confidence in you," he urged. She had taken part in debates before and won prizes too, but she knew she was not the best. He could have asked many others. After much back-and-forth, he revealed the topic: "Competition is better than Cooperation for the success of a business."

Anita, preoccupied with formulas, reagents, species, genus, and exams, felt completely lost. Unfamiliar with the topic, she hesitated. Deshmukh, determined, assured her, "I will write the whole script for you. You need to do nothing, just spare a few hours."

Feeling cornered, Anita reluctantly agreed, but she still had a lingering question, 'why choose her? No professor had ever written a speech for a student, and she could not shake off the feeling that this was more than just a simple favour.' Anita, grateful for Deshmukh's offer, now felt obligated to make up for the past incident.

The town lecture hall buzzed with anticipation as the Chamber of Commerce prepared to host its latest event. Professionals and dignitaries alike filled the seats, eager to absorb the wisdom promised by the evening's speakers.

Among them sat Anita, her heart racing with nervous energy. Since she was not familiar with the topic, she had diligently prepared her speech, understood every word, and broke it into simple language. While her mind yearned to focus on her impending final exams, she found herself immersed in the intricacies of "Co-operation among rivals" and "business by competition."

As the speakers were called to the stage, Anita's gaze searched anxiously for Deshmukh sir, her only support. Her hopes soared when she spotted him entering with the organizers. At first, she thought he had come to wish her luck, but they were quickly dashed as he was escorted to the centre of the dais, designated as the chief guest. He passed by her without a glimmer of recognition, leaving her to face her anxieties alone.

The Secretary of the Chamber introduced the speakers, and Anita barely acknowledged her own name, her mind consumed with the contents of her speech. The secretary went on to introduce the chief guest, 'Mr Deshmukh.' He spoke very highly of him. Everybody clapped when he was awarded a bouquet. Next, the secretary announced that the topic will be opened for debating with Mr. Deshmukh's speech. Deshmukh sir got very agitated. He said, "Isn't this a debate? I will speak at the end, and sum up the discussion. A brief altercation ensued, and the secretary pleaded for him to speak first to accommodate the schedule. He whispered, "Our main guest, a prominent politician, may have to leave early, as he has a flight to catch. We do not want him to miss your speech. Sir, please come first." Reluctantly, Mr. Deshmukh got up and spoke. Anita was too preoccupied with her own speech, to even listen to his complicated words.

Anita was the last to deliver her speech. By the time she came on stage, her confidence grew, with a new found clarity in her thoughts. She was convinced that competition was indeed good for any business, as it improved the quality of goods and services, and increased market share. She spoke emphatically and even dared to refute her previous speaker's points. Her simple yet compelling words, so skilfully presented, appealed to the audience, earning her the loudest applause.

As the event drew to a close Anita was showered with praise from the audience. As she passed through the crowded hall, a lot of people congratulated her. She was in a hurry to get home. She went towards the exit gate to look for her mom, who had also come to attend her lecture. While she was trying to navigate through the crowd, she met a cousin who worked in one of the sponsoring companies.

He said, "The debate went off really well."
'

'Yes,' said she, thinking, I must have been the only spoilsport.

Then he asked, "Do you always speak extempore?"

"Ha! What extempore? I do not know anything about this topic. It was a prepared speech." "But then, how did you manage to demolish all the other's arguments, especially, the chief guests? You refuted each and every argument of his, point by point. You made him look like a fool."

'What? Really?' It was then that the truth dawned on her. So that was the game Deshmukh sir was playing. She now understood why he was insisting that she should deliver this speech. He had prepared a contrary speech himself. He wanted to vindicate a past incident, and if it had not been for the last-minute reversal of the order of speech by the Chamber's secretary, she would have looked like an absolute fool.

Later, for many years, people of the town remembered her as an excellent speaker. Only she knew that this was not true. It was all thanks to Deshmukh sir. It was purely by chance that Deshmukh sir's attempt at revenge, had backfired on him.